The moment the door shut behind Frau Dimpel, Ursula and Berthe began to argue.

"It should be me," Ursula said. "I am the oldest."

"No, it should be me," Berthe said. "Mama needs you in the shop."

"How dare you say so!" Ursula said. "I'm too delicate to work hard all day."

"I deserve to be chosen," Berthe added. "I was made for finer things than selling hats."

"How dare you say so!" Ursula shrieked. She pulled Berthe's hair.

Berthe screamed and pinched Ursula's arm.

Mama clapped her hands. "Hold your tongues! This is too important! One of you will become Frau Dimpel's companion. Then we will have many more rich customers. We will make friends with the rich and be invited to their homes. The Mullers will once again be respectable people."

"Yes, Mama," Ursula said. "That is why it should be me—"

"No, me!" Berthe interrupted.

Nobody paid any attention to me.

**Children of America books
by Jennifer Armstrong**

*Foolish Gretel
Patrick Doyle Is Full of Blarney*

Other books by Jennifer Armstrong

*Steal Away
Hugh Can Do
Chin Yu Min and the Ginger Cat
Little Salt Lick and the Sun King
King Crow
Black-Eyed Susan
The Dreams of Mairhe Mehan*

CHILDREN OF AMERICA

Foolish Gretel

by Jennifer Armstrong
illustrated by Donna Diamond

A STEPPING STONE BOOK

Random House 🏠 New York

http://www.randomhouse.com/

Library of Congress Cataloging-in-Publication Data
Armstrong, Jennifer.
Foolish Gretel / by Jennifer Armstrong ; illustrated by Donna Diamond ;
cover illustration by Bill Dodge.
p. cm. — (Children of America)
"A Stepping Stone book."
SUMMARY: In 1855 in Galveston, Texas, ten-year-old Gretel and her two spoiled,
complaining sisters all hope to be accepted as a companion to Frau Dimpel, the
richest German lady in town.
ISBN 0-679-87287-6 (pbk.) — ISBN 0-679-97287-0 (lib. bdg.).
[1. Sisters—Fiction. 2. German Americans—Fiction. 3. Galveston (Tex.)—Fiction.]
I. Diamond, Donna, ill. II. Title. III. Series: Armstrong, Jennifer. Children of America.
PZ7.A73367Fo 1997 [Fic]—dc20 96-42530
Printed in the United States of America 10 9 8 7 6 5 4 3 2 1

Contents

CHAPTER 1
Muller's Modern Millinery

$\mathcal{O}$nce upon a time, there was a ladies' hat shop in Galveston, Texas. The shop was called Muller's Modern Millinery. It sat on a street called Calle Honig in the shade of a cottonwood tree.

On one side of the hat shop was Schnitzler's Barbershop. On the other side was Kaufmann's Merchandise. A cantina called the Tres Hijas was across Calle Honig. Down the street one way were Braun's Hotel and the water tower. And down the street the

1

other way were Mendoza's Livery Stable and the telegraph office. A customer could see all these places from the sidewalk outside Muller's Modern Millinery, in the shade of the cottonwood tree.

And inside the hat shop were Frau Muller, Ursula Muller, and Berthe Muller.

And me, Gretel Muller.

In our shop were straw hats with pink silk roses on the brim. There were calico bonnets with blue ribbons to tie under the chin. There were silk caps with feathers and all the trimmings. We had every kind of hat for every kind of Texas lady. Mama designed the hats. Ursula made the hats. Berthe sold the hats.

And I swept the floor and did the chores.

"Gretel," Ursula scolded me on the first of July. "Don't stand there daydreaming.

Can't you be useful? I'm working my fingers to the bone! But nobody asks how *I* feel."

Ursula was drinking buttermilk and sitting in a comfortable chair. Her fingers looked fine to me. In fact, she was licking butter off them from the *butterbrot* she was eating.

But I didn't want to be scolded. So I picked up the broom.

There was always sand to sweep up, because Galveston is on the ocean. Galveston, Texas, sits right on the Gulf of Mexico, on a sandy little island.

Galveston was a fine place to be. That was because in almost every direction there was the sea to look at. I loved to walk along the beach to hunt for shells and watch the oyster boats. I thought it would be fun to live on the beach. I would have a fiesta every day, with polkas and dumplings, marzipan and *piñatas*.

"Gretel!" Berthe shouted so loud I dropped my broom. "Don't stand there daydreaming! There isn't another girl as lazy as you in all of Texas! I'm getting a headache watching you be so idle. But nobody asks how *I* feel."

I continued sweeping. There were scraps of pink, yellow, green, and white ribbons on the floor. They reminded me of the long strips of seaweed that wash onto the beach. They reminded me of the coquina shells and sand dollars that roll under the waves.

I could think of nothing finer than enjoying the ocean all day long. How wonderful it would be to sit above the beach on a wide veranda! How peaceful it would be to listen to the waves hit the sand! How magical it would be to watch the pelicans dive for fish and the egrets poke the sand with their long, sharp beaks! How perfect it would be to have a castle by the seashore!

"Gretel!" scolded my mama. "Stop daydreaming! There isn't a more foolish girl in all of Texas!"

"Sorry, Mama," I said. I began sweeping again.

Mama tapped her foot. "I did not *ask* to leave Germany and come to Texas. I did not *ask* your papa to die. I did not *ask* to be a widow with three girls. I did not *ask* to become so poor that I must keep a hat shop! And I certainly did not *ask* to have a simpleton for a daughter!"

"No, Mama," Ursula said. She put marmalade on a *brötchen* and took a big bite. "You did not."

"No, Mama," Berthe agreed. She curled her hair around her finger. "You did not."

"But nobody asks how *I* feel," Mama complained.

I did not want to be scolded anymore. So I took the dustpan and swept the ribbons and scraps into it.

Nobody asked how I felt, either.

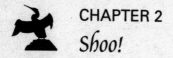

CHAPTER 2
Shoo!

Just then, the bell over the door tinkled. Mama and Ursula and Berthe all looked up. Their eyes were bright and greedy. But when the door opened all the way, Mama and my sisters frowned.

Instead of a rich customer, in walked somebody's slave. She was a very old woman. She had a very old straw basket on her arm and a very old calico bonnet on her head.

"Good afternoon," she said in a very old voice.

"We don't sell hats to slaves," Mama said in her proudest manner.

"So you can just turn right around and leave," Ursula said with her nose in the air.

"And shut the door behind you," Berthe added quickly.

The old woman shook her head. "I only came to ask a little thing. I thought I could get some scraps of ribbon to trim dolly clothes, good ladies."

Ursula's mouth dropped open. "Such a rude and improper question! You can be sure we don't have scraps to give away!"

"Go on now, shoo!" Berthe scolded, waving one hand the way she waved away flies.

The very old woman turned and hobbled out of the shop. The bell tinkled as the door shut behind her.

Ursula, Berthe, and Mama all began talking at the same time.

"Imagine the boldness!"

"A slave coming in here!"

"Slaves will be the ruin of Texas!"

While they were talking, I picked out the longest scraps of ribbon from the pile in the dustpan. Then I slipped outside. Wagons and buggies rattled down dusty Calle Honig. I saw the little old woman hobbling away up the sidewalk.

"Wait!" I called. I ran after her and caught up to her outside the livery stable. A burro tied at the hitching post twitched its long ears at me and said *haw-haw-haw*.

The old woman stopped and turned around. Her old calico bonnet cast a shadow on her face.

"We did have some scraps," I told her.

"My mother and sisters must have forgotten about them."

The little old woman was so old and bent she was almost as small as me. She looked into my eyes. The little burro tried to nibble her straw basket, but she held it out of reach.

"Thank you very much, little miss," she said. "I do appreciate your kindness."

"You're welcome," I replied.

She continued to look into my face, but she didn't speak.

"My family did not mean to be so unfriendly," I told her. "Germans like us don't approve of slavery."

She nodded. "I don't cotton to it myself, missy."

And then she hobbled away.

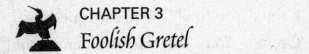

CHAPTER 3
Foolish Gretel

1 waved at Herr Schnitzler, who was leaning against the barber pole outside his shop. Then I waved at Carolina, the cook at Tres Hijas, who was fanning herself outside the cantina. Then I went back into our shop.

Mama and Ursula and Berthe were still complaining. But they stopped speaking when I walked in.

"Where have you been, Gretel?" Mama asked. "You're never around when I need you!"

"I gave the ribbon scraps from the dust-pan to that old woman," I said.

"Gretel! You fool!" Ursula snapped.

"Gretel! You are such a simpleton!" Berthe grumbled.

Mama heaved a heavy sigh. "Gretel, now that woman will come asking for things all the time!"

"And imagine giving good ribbons to a slave!" Ursula said.

"But we were going to throw them away." I couldn't understand why they were so worried about it.

But, after all, my mama and my sisters always found something to complain about. Mama always complained that a hat shop was beneath her. The *floor* was beneath her, but the ceiling of the shop was *above* her, so I didn't understand that.

And Berthe always grumbled that selling hats was low. She sat on a tall stool most of the day, however. She was pretty high up, as far as I could see. So that puzzled me, too.

And Ursula always whined that making hats was common. But ours was the only hat shop in our part of Galveston. So I didn't understand that, either.

Maybe I really was a fool and a simpleton, as they always said. But I didn't understand their complaints. Our hat shop seemed very nice to me. It wasn't the beach, but it was nice. I would have liked to do something besides sweeping and doing errands, though.

Mama began telling stories about the old country. She often reminded us that back in Hamburg, we had been rich and didn't have to run a hat shop. Mama always blamed

Papa for bringing us here and then leaving us all alone.

But he didn't mean to die. It wasn't his fault. I know he didn't want to die. I didn't want him to die, either. He had always called me his little *spätzle*, his dumpling. Nobody called me *spätzle* anymore now that Papa was dead.

"But nobody asked how I felt about it," Mama complained. She picked up a fan and fanned her face.

"Nobody asked how I felt, either," Ursula said.

"And nobody—" began Berthe.

The bell above the door tinkled again. We all looked to see who it was.

In walked fat, dimpled Frau Dimpel, the richest German lady in Galveston.

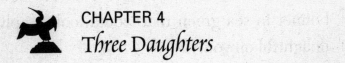

CHAPTER 4
Three Daughters

Mama sprang from her chair with a wide smile. "Welcome, welcome, Frau Dimpel! What a lovely day! What a lovely hat you are wearing. Not one of ours, I see."

"I bought it in New Orleans," Frau Dimpel said.

I pushed a chair forward for her, and Frau Dimpel smiled at me as she sat down. Ursula stuck her tongue out at me, and Berthe pinched my arm.

"What can I show you today?" Mama

asked. She always waited on the very rich customers herself. "We have a lovely new bonnet in sea green that would look simply delightful on you."

Frau Dimpel patted her dimpled cheeks with a lace handkerchief. "Nothing, Frau Muller. No hats today."

"Oh." Mama's smiled drooped. She looked as sad as a wet sombrero.

"I do have a very special request, however," the rich old lady said.

Mama's smile brightened. "Oh?"

"You have daughters," Frau Dimpel began.

Ursula and Berthe both pushed me behind them, out of sight. They stood up straight and tall, and Ursula wiped a *brötchen* crumb from her chin. I watched from behind the counter.

"This is July first, the beginning of the month. I wish to make a new beginning," Frau Dimpel continued. "I am an old widow woman. My children are grown and gone away."

Mama nodded eagerly. *"Ja?"*

"I have an idea that I would like a nice German girl to live with me at my house," Frau Dimpel said. "To have as my companion. To remind me of the old days in Germany. To read to me and play cards with me."

Mama nodded even more eagerly. *"Ja? Ja?"*

Ursula and Berthe stood up even straighter. Their cheeks were pink, and their eyes were as wide as sand dollars.

"I would like to try one of your daughters," Frau Dimpel said. "Each one seems like such a nice young *fräulein*. You choose which one will stay with me. She may come to the house tomorrow morning, and we will see if we get along. Is that satisfactory to you?"

"Oh, *ja, ja!*" Mama gasped. "Yes, indeed!"

Then Frau Dimpel pushed herself out of the chair. I ran forward to open the door, but Berthe grabbed my dress and yanked me back. Then she went to open the door.

Berthe gave Frau Dimpel her prettiest smile.

"Please excuse our foolish Gretel," Mama said. "Berthe will show you out."

"*Auf wiedersehen,*" Frau Dimpel said. "Good day."

"Good day!" Mama said. "*Danke!* Thank you!"

The moment the door shut behind Frau

Dimpel, Ursula and Berthe began to argue.

"It should be me," Ursula said. "I am the oldest."

"No, it should be me," Berthe said. "Mama needs you in the shop."

"How dare you say so!" Ursula said. "I'm too delicate to work hard all day."

"I deserve to be chosen," Berthe added. "I was made for finer things than selling hats."

"How dare you say so!" Ursula shrieked. She pulled Berthe's hair.

Berthe screamed and pinched Ursula's arm.

Mama clapped her hands. "Hold your tongues! This is too important! One of you will become Frau Dimpel's companion. Then we will have many more rich customers. We will make friends with the rich and be invited to their homes. The Mullers will once again be respectable people."

"Yes, Mama," Ursula said. "That is why it should be me—"

"No, me!" Berthe interrupted.

Nobody paid any attention to me.

Mama pointed at Ursula. "My oldest daughter shall go. Do everything you can to please her, Ursula. No matter what she asks!"

Ursula was smirking and grinning at Berthe. "Of course, Mama. I will please Frau Dimpel. I promise."

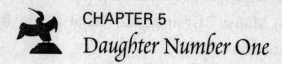

CHAPTER 5
Daughter Number One

In the morning, Ursula put on her Sunday best dress. She put on Mama's best hat. Then she ate a big breakfast and left the shop without even a good-bye.

"It isn't fair," Berthe sniffed. "Ursula gets everything just for being first."

Then she pushed by me. "Gretel, you are always in the way, you little fool! Go sweep something!"

I picked up my broom and began to sweep the floor. How I wished that I could have gone to Frau Dimpel's house. Frau Dimpel lived in a very large white villa overlooking the ocean. From Frau Dimpel's veranda, there would be a wonderful view of the Gulf of Mexico. If I had gone to Frau Dimpel's house, I could have watched the ocean all day.

"Gretel!" Mama scolded. "Stop daydreaming and do some work!"

"Yes, Mama," I said.

So all morning I dusted the shelves and polished the windows and filled the lamps and tended the kitchen stove. Berthe sat on her tall stool with her arms crossed and her lower lip stuck out. Anyone could see she wanted to be at Frau Dimpel's, too. She studied her face in the mirror and tried on different hats to see how pretty she was. And she scolded me, of course, whenever she caught sight of me.

In the middle of the day, I swept the sidewalk in front of our shop, under the shade of the cottonwood tree. Herr Schnitzler came out of his barbershop. He leaned against the barber pole and wiped his forehead. It was very hot.

"I hear your older sister has had good fortune," the barber said to me.

"She's lucky to be the oldest," I said, sweeping sand onto the street.

Herr Schnitzler laughed. "Yes, but in the fairy tales, it is always the youngest daughter who wins the prince or finds the treasure."

I stopped sweeping. "That's true," I agreed. "In fairy tales, there are always three sons or three daughters."

"And the youngest one must pass many tests and trials to win the prize," Herr Schnitzler said. "Good fortune does not

come easy. You must earn it."

"It came easy to Ursula." I continued sweeping. "This is not a fairy tale."

"Frau Dimpel lives in a big villa like a fairy-tale castle," the barber teased. "Whoever lives there will live like a princess."

A hot breeze blew more sand onto the sidewalk. A fairy-tale castle overlooking the beach. That was Frau Dimpel's house, indeed.

But I wasn't there. Ursula was.

I knew it was foolish to daydream about going to Frau Dimpel's house. I was a fool, just as Mama and my sisters always said. I swept the sidewalk clean and then went back inside.

"You certainly took your time," Berthe scolded as the doorbell tinkled behind me. "I've been sitting here in the heat all by myself. But nobody asks how I feel."

"I can get you a drink of water," I said.

"Well, finally someone thinks about me for a change," Berthe said. "If only I could have—"

The bell tinkled again as the door opened. We looked around, and in walked the same old woman in the same old calico bonnet, with the same old straw basket.

"What do you want?" Berthe asked sharply. "We told you yesterday we don't sell to slaves."

"Young misses, it's so hot and I am an old lady," the woman said in a faint voice. "I do feel so hot and tired."

"But you can't come in here just because you're hot!" Berthe snapped. "We're all hot. This is Texas and it's July. Now go on."

Without a word, the old woman turned

and went out. Berthe's words made me feel so bad inside that I felt as if I was being squeezed in a waffle iron. I ran into the back of the shop where our kitchen was. I found a cup and dipped it into our water bucket. Then I ran out the back door, around the side of the shop, and out onto the sidewalk again.

"Wait! Wait!" I called, running after the old woman.

She stopped outside Kaufmann's Merchandise. "Why, thank you so much, little miss. That is very welcome to me."

She sipped the water I gave her and peered into my eyes. Her bonnet cast a deep shadow on her face.

"My sister didn't mean to be unkind," I told her. "We're German, you know. Where we come from, it doesn't get so hot. So

she was very cranky from the heat."

The old woman took another sip of water. "Heat makes me mighty cranky, too." She handed the cup back to me. "Thank you very much."

Just then, something bright caught my

eye. I looked in the display window of Kauf-mann's Merchandise. There was a book of fairy tales lying open on a footstool. A picture showed a wrinkled crone in a black hooded cape speaking to a little girl in the dark pine woods. The caption read: *Thank you, sweet maiden. I will repay your kindness someday.*

Very quickly, I turned to look at the old woman in the calico bonnet.

A buckboard wagon rattled past. A hammer striking the anvil in the livery stable rang out. A sea gull settled on a table in front of Tres Hijas. The smell of salt water and peppery *frijoles* tickled my nose.

But there wasn't a sign of the old woman anywhere on Calle Honig.

CHAPTER 6
Daughter Number Two

*W*hen I went back inside, Berthe began to scold me right away. "I've been waiting and waiting, and I'm so thirsty, Gretel! I thought you were going to bring me some water!"

"I had to give some water to that old woman," I explained.

Berthe's eyes went as round as sand dollars. "What? You gave water to *her*? And left me here dying of thirst? What did I ever do to deserve such a sister?"

And with that, she folded her arms and

sulked so much that she wouldn't take the glass of water when I did get it for her. She sulked all afternoon and tried on all the hats and made me put them away.

Finally, our cuckoo clock struck six. And just as I was about to close up the shop, the door flew open.

Ursula burst in, crying and sobbing and wailing.

Mama ran in from the kitchen, still holding a sausage she was cooking on a fork. "Whatever happened?"

Berthe looked pleased. "Didn't Frau Dimpel like you?"

"No!" Ursula shouted. "She was impossible!"

"Impossible?" Mama asked.

Ursula grabbed the fork from Mama and began to eat the sausage while she spoke.

"She was impossible to please! She was terrible! An ogress!"

"I knew you wouldn't please her," Berthe said with a cheerful smile. "I'm sure *I* could have."

"Don't be so sure! But you can try if you like," Ursula sobbed. She took another bite of sausage. "She said she'll try another sister tomorrow."

Berthe stuck her nose in the air. "Well, I'm sure she'll love me like a daughter."

"Make sure she does," Mama said sternly.

And so, first thing in the morning, away went Berthe in her Sunday dress.

"Good luck," Ursula said in her grouchiest voice. "You'll need it."

"I've always been lucky," Berthe replied. "After all, I was lucky enough to be the pretty one."

She left the shop before Ursula could pull her hair. I stood on our sidewalk, watching her walk up Calle Honig. Berthe was going to the beautiful fairy-tale castle on the beach.

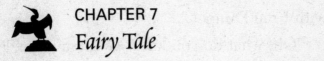

CHAPTER 7
Fairy Tale

*I*t was another hot day. Ursula spent the entire morning nibbling *strudel* and *lebkuchen* and chocolate, and complaining about Frau Dimpel.

"I never met a more difficult person! She acts so kind and friendly when she's here, but that is all false!" Ursula pouted. She sewed a silk flower on a bonnet with large, messy stitches. The flower had *strudel* crumbs in the petals.

"I'm sorry you couldn't stay," I told my

sister. "It must have been just like a fairy tale to be there. I would love to go there and stay with Frau Dimpel."

"Oh, what do you know about anything?" Ursula said with her mouth full of *lebkuchen*. "You're nothing but a fool. Imagine *you* having a chance! If *I* couldn't please Frau Dimpel, *you* certainly couldn't! And don't just stand there—can't you do some work? Am I the only one here who ever does any work? It's not fair!"

I took the broom outside to sweep the sidewalk again. Every day there was more sand to sweep away. Sometimes it made me think that the beach was trying to take over Galveston. Or perhaps the beach was trying to run away from the water. The waves kept rolling and crashing onto the beach, and the sand was trying to escape! I laughed just thinking about it.

"*Guten tag*, Gretel," called Herr Schnitzler.

I waved at him through the open door of the barbershop. "*Guten tag*, Herr Schnitzler! Don't you have any customers today?"

"No, I think maybe it is too hot," the barber said. He joined me on the sidewalk. "Everyone wants to stay in their homes where it is cool. They must all be taking a siesta."

Mama's upstairs window slid open and the shutters flew back. Mama popped her head out like the little bird in our cuckoo clock. "Gretel, don't stand there wasting Herr Schnitzler's time. I am sorry my foolish girl is being a nuisance, Herr Schnitzler."

"Oh, not at all," the barber said with a big smile. "She is my friend."

Mama popped back inside and closed the shutters to keep the sun out of her room.

I was about to tell Herr Schnitzler my idea about the beach running away from the waves when I saw a familiar sight. Down the sidewalk in the blazing sun, walking very slowly, came the same old slave woman. She inched along the sidewalk until she reached the shade of our cottonwood tree.

"Oh, it's mighty hot again today," she sighed. "Mind if I rest here in this shade for a bit?"

Mama opened the shutters and popped her head out the window again. "You can't rest there. You're in the way of our customers going in and out. Move along."

I watched Mama's head pop back out of sight again. We didn't have any more customers than the barber did that day.

I tugged on Herr Schnitzler's sleeve. "Let her sit in one of your barber chairs for a moment, please?"

Herr Schnitzler looked at me. He looked at the little old woman in her old calico bonnet, with her old straw basket over her arm. Then he looked out at the dusty street, where the sun was beating down so hot that even the dust couldn't move.

"Fine. *Ja*. That's fine, you can rest in my shop, old woman."

"Thank you kindly, little miss and big mister," the woman said. She hobbled into the barbershop. She sat down in a big leather barber chair and put her feet on the footrest.

"Mmm-hmm. A comfortable chair," she said with a smile.

She peered at me from under her calico bonnet. She looked at me for such a long

time that I could not help wondering what
she was thinking. Then she nodded her head
once, twice, three times. "Most pleasant rest
I ever had. Thank you."

And with that, she hopped out of the chair and left the barbershop.

"She didn't rest very long," Herr Schnitzler said.

I shook my head. "No, she didn't."

We went to the door to look for her outside.

Two men on palomino horses trotted down the street. A servant shook a dust rag from the porch of Braun's Hotel. A dog barked at a rooster sitting on a post. The smells of sauerkraut and flowering jasmine tickled my nose.

But there was not a sign of the old woman anywhere on Calle Honig.

"Disappeared," Herr Schnitzler said.

I nodded. "I don't know who she is or where she comes from."

Carolina was standing in the doorway of the Tres Hijas, swatting flies on the tables. I waved to her.

"Did you see a little old slave woman? Which way did she go?" I asked Carolina.

Carolina swatted a fly. "I didn't see any-one."

I looked at Herr Schnitzler. He shrugged.

"Magic?" the barber suggested. "Maybe she's a *zauberin,* a witch."

I laughed. "Maybe she is. I wish she'd put a spell on me to let me live at Frau Dimpel's villa."

The barber gave me a wink. "Perhaps she just did."

CHAPTER 8
Daughter Number Three

*W*hen our cuckoo clock struck six, I began to shut the shop for dinner. And once again, the door burst open. Berthe dashed inside, crying tears of anger. "It's not fair!" she howled.

Mama rushed in from the kitchen in the back of the shop. She looked angry. "What happened now?"

Ursula chose a pretzel from the plate on the counter. She looked very pleased. "I know just what happened."

Berthe ripped her bonnet off and threw it on the ground and stamped it with her foot. "Frau Dimpel is an ogress! And nobody ever says a kind thing to me!"

I tapped Berthe's arm. "I'm sorry Frau Dimpel didn't like you," I said.

"Oh, who cares what you're sorry about!" Berthe shrieked. "It's so unfair! I'll never be anywhere important where important people can see me. All my prettiness is going to be wasted!"

Mama paced the shop. Her dress went *flap-flap* about her legs, she walked so hard and fast. "Now what will I do? I had such a wonderful chance, and now it's ruined."

"I'll go, Mama," I said.

"You?" Ursula gasped. She almost choked on her pretzel.

"You?" Berthe groaned.

"Hmm. Gretel?" Mama frowned at me from under her eyebrows.

"I'd try very hard to please Frau Dimpel," I promised. "I'd love to go to her villa."

Berthe and Ursula spun around to face Mama. "Don't send her," Ursula begged.

"If *we* couldn't please Frau Dimpel, *she* never could. She's just a daydreamer," Berthe said.

Mama shook her finger at Ursula and Berthe. "I *will* have *one* of my daughters at Frau Dimpel's house. If you two couldn't do it, I'll try anything. Even Gretel."

"But, Mama!" they cried together.

"If I please her, I'll invite you both to visit," I offered, thinking that would make them happy.

"You goose!" Ursula snapped.

"Fool!" Berthe shouted.

"Enough!" Mama said. "Hold your tongues. You might think about *my* feelings for a change. I can't stand this bickering. Gretel will go to Frau Dimpel's in the morning."

I couldn't help smiling. I was so happy to go.

Of course, I was a little worried about Frau Dimpel. She had always seemed like such a nice lady to me. But Ursula and Berthe both thought she was an ogress.

I wanted to go to the big villa by the ocean, however. So I was willing to face the ogress. After all, Ursula and Berthe could be wrong about Frau Dimpel. I certainly wanted to find out!

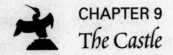

CHAPTER 9
The Castle

*F*irst thing in the morning, I tied my best hat on my head (it was one of Berthe's old bonnets). Then I walked down Calle Honig, past Schnitzler's and the Tres Hijas, past Kaufmann's Merchandise and Mendoza's Livery Stable. I kept walking down Calle Honig until it ended.

Then I turned right and walked until I could see the glimmer of the water ahead of me. Up and down the coast were beautiful seaside villas. I waved to the milkman on his wagon.

"Good morning! I am going to Frau Dimpel's house!" I called to him.

"My, my, my! What a lucky girl," he said. His horse nodded three times, and they went *clop-clop-clop* down the road.

I followed them until I reached the biggest villa of all.

It truly was like a fairy-tale castle, shining white, with flowers blooming along the garden wall. White gravel crunched under my feet as I walked through the garden gate to the door.

The door knocker was in the shape of a dragon. I lifted it carefully and let it fall with a loud *tock!*

I waited. My bonnet strings itched under my chin. A bee buzzed in a pink rose by my arm. A sea gull screeched suddenly. I was at the castle of the ogress!

At last, the doorknob turned. The door slowly opened. And standing on the other side was none other than the old slave woman.

"Good morning, little miss," she said to me. Her eyes twinkled. "My name is Betty, and Mrs. Dimpel says I should bring you right in."

I stared at her in amazement. "You live here?"

"That's right," Betty said. "Now you just pick that little pink rosebud there and bring it to Mrs. Dimpel. She likes flowers."

I was so surprised I didn't know what to say. I picked the rosebud and followed Betty into the villa. The brown-tiled floor made my footsteps echo. Betty led the way up the stairs and then stepped to one side of a closed door.

"Go on in," she whispered to me. "I'll see you in a little while."

Behind that door was the ogress, if Ursula and Berthe were telling the truth. I knocked very softly on the door, and Frau Dimpel's voice called, "Come in!"

Frau Dimpel was sitting at her dressing table, eating her breakfast.

I walked toward her slowly, holding out the rosebud. "For you, Frau Dimpel." I was afraid she might scold me for picking her flower.

But instead of frowning and shouting, Frau Dimpel smiled a wide, dimpled smile.

"*Ach!* So lovely! You have read my mind, *liebchen*. I love to see flowers first thing in the morning. How thoughtful you are!"

"I'm glad you like it, Frau Dimpel," I said. I made a promise to myself to thank Betty for her advice!

"Now, what shall we do together?" Frau Dimpel asked me cheerfully.

"I can read to you, if you like that," I offered.

She threw her hands up and then clapped them with glee. "*Ach!* Perfect. Now run along and find today's newspaper. It should be in the library on the other side of the house. And be quick about it, Gretel! This beautiful morning is slipping away!"

With that, I turned and ran out of the room, down the hall and down the stairs. Then I stopped, unsure what to do.

Now, this house was like many villas. It was a big square with a courtyard in the middle. To reach the library, I had to go all the way around.

But each room was filled with furniture. There were footstools in the way, and large desks and armchairs and sofas and chests and tables and tall candlesticks. There were rugs on the slippery tile floor that skidded under my feet. There were heavy velvet drapes hanging in front of doors that I had to beat my way through.

Each room was more crowded than the last. It was like being in an enchanted forest, where the trees reached out to grab and the roots reached up to trip. I would never get back in time to please Frau Dimpel!

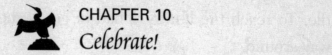

CHAPTER 10
Celebrate!

I was almost out of breath when I reached the library. It was a dark room with thick curtains to keep the hot sun out. A huge wooden table with carved legs stood in the center of the room, and on it was the newspaper. The headline was long and fat.

JULY FOURTH! AMERICA'S BIRTHDAY!
TEXAS CELEBRATES
10 YEARS OF STATEHOOD!

Texas had been a state as long as I had been a person. But I was afraid it would take me another ten years to run all the way around the house again.

As I ran out the door, however, I bumped into Betty. She beckoned me with one crooked finger.

"Don't waste your time going around," she told me. She opened a door onto the courtyard in the center of the house. "Just cut across."

"Thanks, Betty!" I panted.

In a flash, I ran across the courtyard and in through another door. I was on the other side of the house in no time! I ran up the stairs to Frau Dimpel's room.

"Here's the paper," I said.

Frau Dimpel was sipping her coffee and looking out the window at the ocean. She turned to look at me in surprise. "So soon! My goodness, you are so prompt, Gretel.

That is wonderful. I like you very much, Gretel. Very much indeed."

I owed Betty two big thank-yous now. I smiled at Frau Dimpel as I sat down to read her the paper. Ursula and Berthe were wrong. Frau Dimpel wasn't an ogress at all.

But I wasn't sure she wanted me to stay.

As I read the newspaper, Frau Dimpel looked out the window and sipped her coffee. She didn't seem to pay attention. I began to wonder if she disliked my reading.

Then she put her coffee cup down with a clatter.

"I can't bear to be inside any longer," she announced. "I'd like to sit on the veranda and watch the waves. Wouldn't you?"

I couldn't believe my ears. "Oh, yes, Frau Dimpel. I would love it more than anything."

"Good," she said, going to the door. "Why don't we play cards outside?"

"Yes, Frau Dimpel." I followed her. "Shall I get the cards?"

She patted me on the cheek. "Yes, that's a good girl."

"Where are they?" I asked.

Frau Dimpel waved one hand in the air as she started down the stairs. "Somewhere. I'm sure you can find them. Don't take too long!"

She disappeared down the hallway, leaving me at the top of the stairs alone. There was a pack of cards—somewhere. But where? How would I find it in all the jumble of furniture? How would I know which desk or curio cabinet or side table or box to look in? It could take all day!

Even where I was standing there were

chests of drawers and glass-fronted shelves. The whole house was filled with hiding places.

"Where do I start?" I wondered aloud. "How will I ever find it?"

"What are you looking for, little miss?"

Betty was standing at the bottom of the stairs, looking up.

"Oh, Betty! I'm so glad to see you!" I said. I ran down to her. "I have to find a pack of cards, but the house is filled with places to look—and if I don't find them quick enough, I'll never get to stay here and watch the ocean with Frau Dimpel all day! Can't you please help me once more?"

Betty winked. "I believe I can. I do believe I can."

And she reached into the pocket of her dress and pulled out a deck of playing cards.

"You give kindness away, and it always comes back to you," Betty said as she put them in my hand.

I threw my arms around her and gave her a hug. Then I ran to the veranda, where Frau Dimpel sat under a blue-striped awning. Just three steps away was the beach, and the glittering water just beyond.

"Here are the cards," I said with a wide smile.

Frau Dimpel clapped her hands together. "*Ach,* Gretel! Why does your mama always say you are a foolish child? You are a joy to me! Your sisters only wanted to sit and have sweet cakes and look in my mirrors! Now, I am a quiet old woman. I do very little except watch the waves and read. But would you like to stay here with me and keep me company? Of course, you can visit your mama and your sisters any time you wish."

I sat down beside her and began to shuffle the cards. A pelican dove into the water of the gulf. An egret poked its sharp beak into the sand. The waves poured onto the beach like cream.

"*Danke*, Frau Dimpel," I told her. "I would like it very much."

And we lived happily ever after in the castle by the sea.

A Little Bit of History

The first Germans to arrive in America came in 1683 and settled in Germantown, Pennsylvania. They have continued arriving in every century since then, playing a large part in the American Revolution and many other important events in our history. Some of them moved for religious reasons, because Protestants and Catholics fought wars against each other in Germany. Some came because land was scarce back home. Some came because they wanted to live in a democratic country where they could vote.

In the middle of the 1800s, it became harder and harder for Germans to find land, houses, and jobs at home. There were many wars throughout Europe in the 1840s, and that began a new wave of immigration to the United States. Gretel Muller's family decided to move in 1850.

We usually think of German immigrants moving to the Midwest. But many thousands of them moved to Texas. There was even a special group called the Texas Society for the Care of German Immigrants. It was also known as the *Aldesverein*.

When Texas separated from Mexico in 1836, it became a country called the Republic of Texas, with its capital at Galveston. It did not charge tax on its land, which was one reason Germans moved there. In 1845,

Texas became the 28th state. It was a southern slave state.

Most German immigrants were opposed to slavery. Germans had been opposed to slavery in America since 1688, when the Germantown settlers wrote an important anti-slavery document. Like Gretel's family, however, some immigrants opposed slavery but were unkind and unfriendly to slaves. Some even owned slaves, like Frau Dimpel. Fortunately, the Civil War (1861–1865) ended slavery throughout the South, including Texas.

Because Texas was originally part of Mexico, there have always been many Mexican influences. When Gretel and her family moved to Texas, they would have had to learn both English and Spanish.

America has been influenced by the Germans in many ways. The Germans introduced Americans to the Christmas tree and Santa Claus. We go to kindergarten, we eat pretzels and pumpernickel bread. We like sauerkraut on our frankfurters. And of course, all children know the fairy tales of the Brothers Grimm.

 *Glossary*

barber pole A red-and-white-striped pole outside many barbershops.
buckboard wagon A large, open four-wheeled carriage pulled by horses.
curio An unusual article or object of art.
livery stable A "parking lot" for horses.
millinery shop A women's hat shop.
ogress A monstrous or cruel woman.
veranda A large, open porch, usually extending across the front and sides of a house.

Spanish words

burro (BOO-roh) A little donkey.
calle (KIE-yay) A street.
cantina (kan-TEE-nuh) A small restaurant.

coquina (ko-KEE-nuh) A little clam that comes in pastel colors.

fiesta (fee-ES-tuh) A party.

frijoles (free-HO-lays) Beans.

palomino (pal-uh-MEE-noh) A horse with a golden coat, a white mane and tail, and white markings on the face and legs.

piñata (pin-YAH-tuh) A papier-mâché animal filled with toys or candy. It is hung from a tree at parties and hit with a stick until the goodies fall out.

siesta (see-ES-tuh) A nap in the hot, hot middle of the day.

sombrero (som-BREH-roh) A broad-brimmed, high-crowned hat made of straw or felt.

tres hijas (trace EE-hahs) Three daughters.

villa (VEE-yah) A large house.

German words

ach (akh) Oh.

auf wiedersehen (ouf VEE-duhr-zay-uhn) Good-bye.

brötchen (BROTE-shuhn) A little loaf of bread; a roll.

butterbrot (boo-tuhr-braht) A slice of bread and butter.

danke (DAHN-kuh) Thank you.

frau (frou) Mrs.; a married woman.

fräulein (FROY-line) Miss; a girl or young woman.

guten tag (GOOT-n tahg) Good day.

herr (hair) Mr.; sir.

honig (HOH-nig) Honey.

ja (yah) Yes.

lebkuchen (LABE-koo-khuhn) A hard, chewy or brittle cookie.

liebchen (LEEB-shuhn) Darling; sweetheart.

marzipan (MAR-zuh-pahn) A candy made from sugar and almond paste that can be molded into different shapes.

polka (POLE-kuh) A lively dance.

sauerkraut (SOU-uhr-krout) Pickled shredded cabbage.

spätzle (SHPET-suhl) A dumpling.

strudel (SHTROOD-l) A baked pastry, usually filled with fruit or cheese.

zauberin (TSOU-bare-een) A witch.

About the Author

JENNIFER ARMSTRONG lived in Switzerland as a girl and visited nearby Germany many times on school holidays. "I was sure that Rumpelstiltskin and Rapunzel and the rest lived somewhere in Germany. The characters in Grimm's fairy tales were like neighbors. But I never met them except in books."

She still loves fairy tales and has written many new tales as picture books. Armstrong has also written historical chapter books and novels for children, including *Steal Away, The Dreams of Mairhe Mehan,* and *Black-Eyed Susan.* She lives in Saratoga Springs, New York, with her husband, and, unlike Gretel, has just one older sister.